# Magic Kitten

## Moonlight Mischief

*To Misty, my grumpy*
*blue-cream Persian girl.*

GROSSET & DUNLAP
Published by the Penguin Group
Penguin Group (USA) Inc., 375 Hudson Street,
New York, New York 10014, USA
Penguin Group (Canada), 90 Eglinton Avenue East, Suite 700,
Toronto, Ontario M4P 2Y3, Canada
(a division of Pearson Penguin Canada Inc.)
Penguin Books Ltd., 80 Strand, London WC2R 0RL, England
Penguin Group Ireland, 25 St. Stephen's Green, Dublin 2, Ireland
(a division of Penguin Books Ltd.)
Penguin Group (Australia), 250 Camberwell Road,
Camberwell, Victoria 3124, Australia
(a division of Pearson Australia Group Pty. Ltd.)
Penguin Books India Pvt. Ltd., 11 Community Centre,
Panchsheel Park, New Delhi—110 017, India
Penguin Group (NZ), 67 Apollo Drive, Rosedale, North Shore 0632, New Zealand
(a division of Pearson New Zealand Ltd.)
Penguin Books (South Africa) (Pty.) Ltd., 24 Sturdee Avenue,
Rosebank, Johannesburg 2196, South Africa

Penguin Books Ltd., Registered Offices:
80 Strand, London WC2R 0RL, England

Text copyright © 2006 Sue Bentley. Illustrations copyright © 2006 Angela Swan.
Cover illustration copyright © 2006 Andrew Farley. First printed in Great Britain in
2006 by Penguin Books Ltd. First published in the United States in 2009 by Grosset &
Dunlap, a division of Penguin Young Readers Group, 345 Hudson Street, New York, New
York 10014. GROSSET & DUNLAP is a trademark of Penguin Group (USA) Inc. Printed
in the U.S.A.

Library of Congress Control Number: 2008053747.

ISBN 978-0-448-45061-2                    10 9 8

# Magic Kitten

## Moonlight Mischief

# SUE BENTLEY

Illustrated by Angela Swan

Grosset & Dunlap

# ★ Prologue ★

A flash of dazzling white light and silver
sparkles crossed the sky. Where the young
white lion had stood just a moment ago,
now crouched a tiny kitten with long,
sandy fur. The sun beat down on a grove
of nearby thorn trees.

An old, gray lion ran up to the kitten
and bowed his head. "Prince Flame!
The magic worked again! You have
transformed yourself again to hide in this
kitten disguise. But you shouldn't be here.
Your uncle Ebony still searches for you,"
Cirrus growled.

The kitten trembled but he stood up and shook himself. "One day I will fight Ebony for the kingdom he has stolen from me!" he meowed bravely.

Cirrus nodded his shaggy head and his eyes glowed with affection. "We all hope that day is soon, Prince Flame. But first you must grow strong and wise. Go far from here and hide in the other world once more, where you will be safe. Then return, to claim the Lion Throne."

"Nowhere is safe from my uncle's spies . . ." Flame broke off as a deep terrifying roar rang out.

Cirrus moved quickly, shielding the tiny kitten with his body.

A huge, black, adult lion came from

behind a thorn tree. It lifted its head and sniffed the air. Suddenly it stiffened and its cruel eyes fastened on Cirrus.

"Ebony has your scent! Quickly, Flame! Go now!" Cirrus yowled urgently.

The adult lion snarled and bared its enormous teeth. It leaped forward and bounded toward Cirrus. Its mighty paws pounded the grass, and the ground beneath Flame's tiny paws shook.

Silver sparks glittered in Flame's long sandy fur and the kitten meowed as he felt the power building inside him. All sound faded. The ground seemed to sink beneath him and he felt himself falling. Falling . . .

# Chapter
# *ONE*

Eve Dawson stared gloomily out of the car as it came to a halt on the road. There was a wooden sign by the front gate, which read "Ross's Kennel. Open All Year." A basket of cheerful purple and yellow pansies hung below the sign.

"Well, here we are. Right on time," Mrs. Dawson said brightly, glancing at her watch. "Sally has arranged for someone to meet us here with a key."

*Maybe they'll have lost the key and we*

*can go back home*, Eve thought, getting out.

She stood with crossed arms, looking up at the gray stone house.

Mr. Dawson came over and put his arm around Eve's shoulder. "Cheer up! It's only for a few days, while Sally's away. You might even enjoy yourself."

"Oh, right. Cleaning up tons of smelly cat litter! My favorite way to spend my spring break vacation. Not!" Eve muttered.

A few weeks ago, Eve reluctantly agreed to come and help her mom and dad look after the kennel only because she really liked the owner, Sally Ross. Sally was an old school friend of her mom's. She never forgot Eve's birthday and always sent amazing Christmas presents in the mail. But Eve couldn't help thinking about her own school friends who would be meeting up and having fun without her. She just wished the kennel was closer to home.

The door of a cottage across the road opened. A young woman, a girl, and a little boy came out. The woman waved as they all crossed the road and came up the driveway.

"Hello, everyone! I'm Jo Hinds, Sally's assistant," the woman said cheerfully. "I've got a set of keys for you. I'll let you in and show you around. This is my daughter Alison and my son Darren."

"Nice to meet you all," Mr. and Mrs. Dawson said.

Darren smiled up at Eve, his big blue eyes sparkling. He had curly blond hair and a sweet face and was clutching a bright-red fire engine. Eve smiled at the cute little boy who looked about four years old.

Alison was tall with long brown

hair and looked about twelve. She had a pretty face, which was spoiled by her sulky expression. She glanced at Eve. "What's your name?" she asked abruptly.

"I'm Eve," Eve said, smiling. "It's nice to meet . . ." she began, but the older girl had already turned her back.

Alison stuck her hands in her jeans' pocket and slouched after her mom who was showing Eve's parents through a side gate.

Eve stared at the older girl as she walked away, surprised at her unfriendliness. But she shrugged and followed her. At the back of the house, a big L-shaped extension took up most of the garden. Near the house there was a tiny patio with a table and chairs. Pots of plants stood in front of a fence. From the faint sounds in the background, Eve guessed that the cats' cages must be behind the fence.

"I'll put the teapot on the stove," Jo said, once they were all in the light, modern kitchen. "I've made some sandwiches. Maybe we could all have lunch after you've had a quick look around."

Mrs. Dawson smiled. "Thanks, Jo. That's very thoughtful of you."

While her parents chatted with Jo,
Eve wandered into the hall and then into
the living room. It looked cozy, with red
curtains and bookcases against one wall.
There were two sofas and a bright rug in
front of a huge stone fireplace. Polished
horse brasses hung above the fireplace.

She heard someone come in
behind her.

"It's not bad, is it? If you can stand
looking at all those boring books." Alison
walked across the room. She threw
herself onto one of the sofas and lay on
her back, dangling her legs over one side.

"Actually, I really like reading," Eve
said.

"It's okay, I guess, if there's nothing
else to do," Alison said.

"Where are you, Alison? Wait for me!" called a voice.

Darren dashed into the room. He sprawled on the rug and ran his toy fire engine back and forth. "Brr-rrrum! Brr-rrrm!" he said loudly.

Eve smiled. "Darren seems really sweet."

"Huh! You don't know him," Alison muttered.

Just then Jo poked her head around the door. "I'm going to take the Dawsons into the office and show them where things are. Why don't you take Eve up to see her bedroom, Alison? And could you keep an eye on Darren, please?"

"If I have to," Alison said under her breath. As soon as her mom went out, she quickly swung her feet around and got up. She glanced at Darren who was completely engrossed in his game. "Come on, quick! We'll leave him there," she whispered to Eve.

"Are you sure . . . ?" Eve hesitated.

"Yes, I am! Hurry up!" Alison grabbed her arm and pulled her into the hall.

Eve couldn't help laughing as they raced up the stairs together. Alison darted

into a bedroom, pulled Eve in behind
her, and closed the door.

"That little pest won't find us in
here," she said, grinning.

Eve felt a little mean for hiding
from Darren, but she didn't want to say
anything and risk upsetting Alison. She
seemed to be trying to be friendly now.
Eve looked around at her bedroom. The
walls were yellow and the curtains and
duvet were in cheerful stripes of yellow
and white. The room seemed filled with
sunshine. From the window, she could
see over the patio fence to the rows of
outdoor cages.

"This is a great room. You can see
the yard and cat cages from up here,"
Eve said excitedly.

"Glad you like it. Mom and I cleaned the house yesterday. I did all the vacuuming by myself," Alison said. "Darren played with his toys, as usual. Mom never makes him do anything."

Eve thought Darren looked a little young to do chores, but she didn't say so. "Does your mom come in every day?" she asked.

"Not usually, but she's going to while you're here." Alison made a face. "She's going to help with feeding the cats and stuff, too. That's why I have to help her. It's a real pain. I'm never going to be able to see my friends."

"I know what you mean," Eve said with feeling. "I keep thinking of all my friends back at home. Maybe *we*

could go out for a pizza or rent a movie
sometime?"

Alison rolled her eyes. "If I get
desperate! I'm not that into hanging out
with younger kids."

"Fine!" Eve said, feeling her face
grow hot. She hated the way she blushed
when she was embarrassed or annoyed.
It seemed like a waste of time trying to
make friends with Alison. She quickly
turned on her heel. "I'm going to see
what Mom and Dad are doing."

Alison stood there, staring after her.
"Hey! I didn't mean . . ." she began.

"Forget it!" Eve called over her
shoulder, already on her way downstairs.

In the kitchen, Eve saw that the door
into the kennel office was open. She

found her mom sitting at a computer, while Jo explained about the files and records. Her dad stood by, looking confused.

Mr. Dawson winked at Eve as she came in. Eve smiled back at him. Her dad was useless with computers!

"Bedroom okay?" her dad asked. "How are you getting along with Alison?"

"Okay," Eve said, still feeling hurt from the unfriendly comment. "My bedroom's great. What's through here?"

"That's the storeroom. Go and take a look. It leads to the outdoor cages where the cats live." He grinned. "Meeting the cats will definitely put a smile on your face after pouting the whole car ride here!"

Eve put her hands on her hips.
"Da-ad! I'm not a baby anymore! I'm
going to be eleven on my next birthday!
And I've got an even better cure. How
about letting me have my own pet
kitten?"

He chuckled, twinkling at her. "Nice

try! What is this, pester power?" he teased.

"You bet!" Eve laughed and gave her dad a playful shove. He could always cheer her up. And one day she *was* going to have a pet cat. She just needed to work on him a bit harder.

She went through the storeroom and straight outside to the rows of mesh wire cages. They all had inside sleeping places and heat lamps for cold weather. In one cage, a Siamese cat was curled up in its bed. In another, Eve saw two kittens playing with a toy.

Suddenly, out of the corner of her eye, Eve saw a flash of bright white light. She spun around to see what seemed to be an empty cage glowing among all the others.

Eve frowned. What was that? Curious,

she went to have a closer look.

"Oh!" she gasped.

There, on the concrete floor crouched a gorgeous, tiny kitten with long, sand colored fur and the brightest emerald eyes Eve had ever seen. Its fur and whiskers seemed to be glowing with a thousand tiny sparkles of light.

Eve blinked hard as she took a step closer, but the sparkles seemed to have died down and just the tiny, sand colored kitten remained. Eve shook her head— she must have been seeing things. She was very tired from the long car journey, after all.

She bent down to pet the kitten. "Hello. Where did you come from? And how did you get inside that cage?"

The kitten's little body trembled, but it sat up and looked straight at Eve with wide, scared, green eyes. "I come from far away and my enemies are looking for me. Can you help me hide, please?" it meowed.

# Chapter
# *TWO*

Eve stared at the kitten in utter amazement. Now she was hearing things as well as seeing things! She started to back off toward the house, but stopped. The tiny kitten looked so alone.

"You . . . you didn't really just speak to me, did you?" Eve stammered.

There was a pause and the sand colored kitten blinked slowly. "Yes, I did. I am Prince Flame." Some of the fear seemed to fade from his big emerald eyes. "Who are you and what is your name?"

"I'm Eve. Eve Dawson. I'm . . .
um . . . looking after this kennel with
my mom and dad," Eve answered
hesitantly. Her curiosity began to get the
better of her shock. "Did you say *Prince*
Flame?"

Flame nodded and lifted his tiny, sand
colored head proudly. "I am heir to the
Lion Throne. My uncle Ebony has stolen
my throne and rules in my place. His
spies are searching for me. They want to
kill me."

"Kill you?" Eve gasped. Flame was so
tiny and helpless-looking. She felt a burst
of protectiveness toward him. "If any of
those cats come here they'll have to deal
with me first!" She had a sudden thought.
"Is your uncle a kitten like you?"

"No. Ebony is enormous and very strong," Flame growled softly, showing his little sharp teeth for the first time. "But he and I are not cats."

"Then what . . . ?"

There was a blinding silver flash. Eve couldn't see anything for a second and then her sight cleared. Where the cute kitten had been now stood a majestic, young, white lion.

Eve gasped and took a big step backward.

Flame's fierce emerald eyes softened. "Do not be afraid," he said in a deep, velvety roar. There was another flash and Flame was a cute, sand colored kitten with long, silky fur again.

"Well, I hope I never meet your

uncle!" Eve said in a shaky voice. "Come on, Flame. Let's hide. I'll take you into the house."

As she bent down and picked Flame up, a few sparks from his fur tingled against her fingers before they went out. "Just wait until I tell Mom and Dad all about you!"

"No! You must tell no one my secret." Flame reached up and put a paw on her chest. He had a serious expression on his tiny face. "Please promise, Eve."

"All right. I promise. I'll just say you're a stray and I'm going to take care of you," Eve agreed disappointedly.

Her dad would have been as amazed and excited as she was about Flame, but a promise is a promise. She just hoped she could keep Flame's secret with so many people coming and going at the kennel.

Flame rubbed the top of his head against her arm and began purring loudly. "That is good. Thank you, Eve."

★

"I'm sorry, but keeping Flame is
out of the question," Mrs. Dawson said
firmly. She had laid down the book she'd
been reading. "We've got more than fifty
cats to take care of, Eve. You can't really
expect us to let you keep another one!"

Eve stared at her mom in utter
dismay. "But I *have* to take care of
Flame. He's in danger of . . ." She
stopped in horror, realizing that she
had been about to reveal Flame's
secret. ". . . of starving or getting run
over or even freezing to death!" she
rushed on.

Her mom sighed. "Don't be so
dramatic, Eve! A stray could be carrying
cat flu or anything. The responsible thing

to do is contact the local pet shelter."

Eve felt tears of frustration pricking her eyes. She tried desperately to think

of something to change her mom's mind. "What if we got Flame checked out by a vet? If he's given a clean bill of health, can I keep him?"

Mrs. Dawson shook her head. "I don't know . . ."

"Oh, please, Mom. You know I've wanted a cat of my own for so long! If you let me keep Flame, I'll never ask you for anything ever again! He can sleep in my room and everything. You'll hardly even know he's here!"

Her dad came into the living room with a newspaper under his arm. "What's going on? And where did that gorgeous little kitten come from? I haven't noticed him before."

"I just found him . . ." Eve began.

Mary Dawson put a hand on her daughter's arm. She explained the situation, while her husband listened patiently. There was a pause when she'd finished speaking. Eve thought she might burst with the tension of waiting for her dad to speak.

"I guess it wouldn't hurt to get the little guy checked out, would it?" Jim Dawson said thoughtfully, at last.

"Yes!" Eve put Flame down on the sofa. She flew across the room and hugged her dad, silently promising herself to laugh at all his awful jokes for the next ten years. "Mom?" Eve said in her best pleading voice, hoping desperately her mom would follow her dad.

Mary Dawson nodded. "All right. We'll take Flame to the vet first thing tomorrow. But that doesn't mean you can keep him. We'll talk about it again later."

"Okay, Mom," Eve said meekly, picking Flame up again. She bent her head and whispered in his ear. "Don't worry, she'll let you stay. I know it." Turning back to her parents, she said in a louder voice, "I'm going to get some food for Flame and make him a bed in my room."

★

Eve woke the following morning to the sound of loud purring in her ear.

She turned over and gave Flame a cuddle. His beautiful, long, sand colored fur was the softest thing she had ever touched. "Did you sleep well?" she asked him.

Flame's emerald eyes glowed with contentment. "Very well, thank you. I feel safe here with you," he meowed.

Eve tried not to think about the
vet. What if he found that Flame had
something wrong with him? Or even
realized that Flame wasn't from this
world? She felt her heart turn over at the
thought of not being allowed to take care
of the gorgeous kitten.

Eve got up to feed Flame. She felt too anxious to eat much breakfast herself, but managed half a slice of toast.

"Shut Flame in your bedroom for now," her mom said afterward. "I don't want him near any of the cats until he's been to the vet."

Eve didn't argue. She didn't want to do anything to make her mom change her mind. "Sorry, Flame. It's only for a little while," she said, petting his little soft ears as she put him on the duvet.

Flame nodded. "Okay. I will stay here." He twitched his silky tail and settled down for a nap.

Eve helped her dad with the morning chores, while her mom dealt with a couple of new bookings. Jo,

Alison, and Darren arrived just as Eve
was washing her hands at the sink in the
storeroom. Alison came up to her.

"Hi, Eve," Alison said brightly,
coming straight over. "Sorry I was in a
bad mood yesterday. I . . ." she broke off
as Eve looked past her.

Eve had spotted her dad coming
toward her with a pet carrier in one hand
and his car keys in the other. "All set,
then? Go and get Flame, honey."

Alison frowned. "Who's Flame?"

"My kitten!" Eve called as she dashed
up to her bedroom.

Alison stood looking at Eve with
a scowl on her face. "You just can't
apologize to some people," she grumbled.

When Eve came back down with

Flame to put him inside the carrier,
Alison was nowhere in sight. "Sorry,
but you have to travel inside this," she
whispered to the tiny kitten as she made
him comfortable.

It was only a short journey to the
clinic, but Eve's stomach clenched with
nerves. When her name was called, she
took Flame into the treatment room and
carefully lifted him onto the table.

"Hello there, little fellow," the vet
said in a friendly voice. "What seems to
be the trouble?" he asked Eve.

"I think he's fine. But Mom says
Flame has to have a full checkup," Eve
explained.

The vet smiled. "Flame does look
like a perfectly healthy kitten, but it's

always good to make sure." He checked Flame's fur for flea dirt, and then looked at his teeth, nose, eyes, and under his tail. "He's got a nice, fat tummy, just like a kitten should have."

Flame squirmed and meowed indignantly at the vet's words.

Eve bit back a grin. She was sure that Flame was dying to protest at being told he had a fat tummy and she wondered what the vet would say if he knew he was examining a royal magic kitten!

"Well, Flame's a picture of health," the vet said finally.

On the way out, Flame licked his paw and washed his face. "I could have told him that!" he purred to Eve, still looking quite annoyed.

Eve gave him a big cuddle.

Flame purred contentedly in the car
on the way back as Eve pet him through
the mesh of the pet carrier.

"You're really in love with that kitten,
aren't you?" her dad said.

"Yes, I am. I love him to bits, Dad,"
Eve said. "It already feels like Flame's
lived with me forever."

"Oh, well. Now he's got a clean bill
of health, I think we might let him stay."

Convincing her dad to let her keep
Flame was only half the battle. Eve bit
her lip. "But . . . what about Mom?"

"You leave her to me," her dad said
with a wink.

# Chapter
# *THREE*

The following afternoon, Eve was curled up with Flame on the sofa. A big log fire burned in the grate. Leaves, whipped up by the breeze, were blowing past outside the window.

"I guess I should go help Mom and Dad," she said, reluctantly pushing herself to her feet. "I'd rather stay here with you, Flame. But I need to be on my best behavior for the next couple of days. Just to be on the safe side with Mom."

Flame stretched, then yawned, showing his sharp little teeth. "I will come with you."

Eve heard Jo's angry voice floating out of the kitchen. She looked inside to see if her mom or dad were in there.

"What have I told you about keeping an eye on Darren, Alison? It's a good thing he only ate a few cat treats. Just imagine if he'd opened a can of cat food!" Jo fumed.

Eve saw Alison leaning against the sink with folded arms, a sulky look on her face. "That's it, blame me! Everything that goes wrong around here is always my fault!" she grumbled.

Darren sat at the kitchen table drinking a glass of orange juice. He shot

Eve a sneaky grin, looking none the worse for apparently having eaten food meant for the cats.

Eve gave Alison a sympathetic smile before going off to find her parents.

Mr. Dawson was in the storeroom. He smiled when he saw Flame trotting along behind Eve. "I have to admit,

Flame will be an unusually cute addition to the family. Just don't let him get under anyone's feet when we're busy, young lady."

"I won't," Eve promised, still feeling grateful to her dad. Whatever he had said to change her mom's mind about keeping Flame, it had worked like a dream. Flame was now an official member of the family!

Mr. Dawson was loading a wheelbarrow with litter trays and clean cat litter. He wore a bright-red plastic apron, pink rubber gloves, and blue boots.

"What *are* you wearing?" Eve said, holding both hands over her mouth to stop laughing.

"What?" Her dad looked down at himself. "It's all the rage on the Paris

catwalks this year. Get it—catwalks?" he
said, trying to keep a straight face.

Eve shook her head slowly as she got
herself an apron and gloves. "That's a
terrible joke!"

She and Flame headed outside to the
cages, while her dad walked behind them
with the wheelbarrow. Even the boring
task of changing litter trays was bearable
with Flame for company.

Eve made friends with all kinds of
cats. There were Siamese with blue
eyes, Persians with fluffy coats and flat
faces, and all sizes and colors of ordinary
household pets.

Flame nudged Eve's leg and looked up
at her with troubled eyes. "What have
these cats done wrong, to be punished by

being kept in these cages?" he meowed sadly.

Eve smiled gently as she bent down to pet him. "They aren't being punished. We're taking care of them for their owners while they're away. The cats only stay here for a couple of weeks and then they go back home."

Flame looked very relieved. His tiny face brightened when Eve stopped by a cage with a big ginger and white cat inside. The cat's name, Oscar, was on a card attached to the mesh.

Eve bent down and pushed a finger through the mesh. "Hello, Oscar. You're handsome!" she said in a gentle friendly voice.

Oscar laid back his ears, bared his

teeth, and hissed loudly. He swung his thick tail back and forth.

"Okay! I get the message!" Eve backed off with a smile. "We'll come back and see him when he's in a better mood," she said to Flame.

Flame gave a friendly little meow and poked his nose through Oscar's mesh. "Is something wrong? May I help you?" he purred.

Eve waited expectantly, to see if Oscar would respond. It would be so amazing if Flame's magic would make *him* able to speak, too. But the big ginger cat just glared and then turned away.

Flame sighed with disappointment. "It seems my kind do not have the power to speak to cats in this world." He glanced once more at Oscar before following Eve to the next cage.

★

Eve had finished helping her dad and was washing her hands in the storeroom when her mom popped her head around the door. "Eve!" she called. "Would you mind running out for a jar of coffee? We just ran out."

"No problem!" Eve jumped at
the chance of exploring the village
and stores. She grabbed her coat and bag
and was ready in two minutes flat.

"Come on, Flame. Let's go," she
said, slinging her bag over her shoulder
and holding the side gate open for him.

Flame scampered ahead of Eve. His
sand colored fur blew about in the wind
as he chased the leaves tumbling along
the path.

As they reached the supermarket, Eve
had a sudden thought. "They don't allow
animals inside. You'd better get in my
bag." She bent down so Flame could
jump in.

Once inside, she picked up a basket
and started looking for the coffee. She

wandered up and down, checking the
shelves and enjoying showing Flame new
things. As she drew near the toy section,
she heard a child shouting.

"No! I want one *now*!"

The voice sounded familiar. Eve
peeked around a corner and saw Darren

and Alison near a tall display of boxed toy cars. Darren was stamping his feet and yelling.

Alison had a shopping cart loaded with groceries. Her back was turned to Eve. "Stop acting like a two-year-old, Darren! You know you can't have one," she said, wheeling her cart around the end of the shelf. "Come on. I'm going to pay for all of this now."

"I don't care!" Darren yelled, staying behind in the empty aisle. He stretched forward and grabbed a box from near the bottom of the display.

Eve gasped as the huge pile of boxes shifted and the entire display slowly leaned toward Darren.

Time seemed to stand still. Eve felt a

strange warm tingling up her spine. She looked down at her bag. Flame's head was sticking out. His silky fur was fizzing with a shower of silver sparkles and his whiskers crackled with electricity.

Eve tensed. It felt like something very strange was about to happen.

# Chapter
# *FOUR*

Lifting a tiny paw out of Eve's bag, Flame sent a fountain of sparks toward the collapsing display.

Suddenly there was a faint *pop!* and Eve saw the heavy toy boxes magically transform into a shower of colorful glittering feathers, which drifted down harmlessly around Darren.

"Cool!" Darren clapped his hands. He kicked the feathers around and jumped up and down on them, completely forgetting about the toy cars. With sparkling feathers

stuck all over him, Darren ran after
Alison, shouting, "Come and look at this,
Alison. Come and look!"

Eve gasped. What if anyone saw
what had just happened? Flame might be
found out! She would have to warn him.
"Flame, you've got to . . ."

But before Eve could finish, Flame

waved a sand colored paw at the
enormous pile of glittering feathers
drifting across the shop floor. In another
flash of silver sparks every single feather
disappeared. The tall display of boxed cars
stood neatly in their place.

Eve stared in amazement as the
sparkles in Flame's silky fur gradually
faded away. "Phew! That was close. You
were amazing, Flame!"

"I am glad to help you, Eve," Flame
meowed, looking up at her with his big
emerald eyes.

Eve found the jar of coffee and went
to pay for it. Alison and Darren were
still at the checkout. Alison was packing
groceries into plastic bags, while Darren
looked out of the window.

"Can I help you do that?" Eve said.

Alison glanced up. She looked fed up. "You can if you want."

Eve packed a bag and then carried it outside with Alison. Neither of them spoke. Darren took a ball out of his pocket and bounced it down the path.

"I heard Darren having a temper tantrum in the store," Eve said, to break the awkward silence.

Alison made a face. "That's nothing new. He always acts up if he can't have something he wants."

"What a brat!" Eve said sympathetically.

Alison nodded. "I suppose he's no worse than other kids. But he drives me crazy!" Her face suddenly broke into a

genuine smile. "Thanks for helping me
with the bags."

"No problem," Eve replied, returning
her smile.

Alison looked thoughtful. "Mom said
I could go to the movies tomorrow. My
friends are busy, so I was going by myself.
Do you want to come?"

"That would be great. I'll ask Mom and Dad if it's okay," Eve said, really happy that Alison had invited her. Maybe they could be friends after all, even after getting off to a bad start.

Suddenly Alison stiffened. "Your bag! It just moved!"

Eve chuckled. "Flame's inside. He comes everywhere with me, but I thought they wouldn't let me in the store with him." She opened her bag and lifted Flame out.

"Oh, isn't he swe-eet!" Alison crooned. She scratched Flame gently under the chin. "Look at his gorgeous silky fur and green eyes! That's nice being able to bring your own cat with you from home."

Eve was trying to decide how to avoid

complicated explanations when Darren
came running up. He had spotted Flame.

"I want to hold the kitten!" he
demanded.

Alison looked doubtful.

"It's okay, he can. Flame won't mind,"
Eve said, putting him into Darren's arms.

"Be very gentle and don't squeeze him," Alison told her brother.

"Aw, he's cute! I want a kitten like this." The little boy hunched over, cuddling Flame and gently petting the top of his head. Flame wriggled around and whined softly.

Eve felt uneasy. What was wrong with Flame? He didn't seem to be feeling comfortable with Darren. As the little boy glanced up at Eve, she saw his blue eyes flash with mischief.

Alarm bells went off in her head. "I'll take Flame back now, Da . . ."

But it was too late. Clutching Flame tightly to his chest, Darren ran down the street and straight into a children's playground!

# Chapter
# *FIVE*

Eve shot after Darren. She ran into
the playground, which was crowded with
moms and children. She spotted Darren
at the back of a line of little kids all
climbing a slide. Darren was two steps
from the top when he slipped and almost
toppled backward.

"Oo-er!" he cried, dropping Flame
and grabbing at the handrail.

"Meee-ow-ow!" Flame gave a howl
of fear as he managed to cling on to the
edge of the steps with his front paws. His

back legs scrambled for a foothold, but
he was gradually slipping.

Eve realized that Flame couldn't
use magic in the crowded playground
without giving himself away. He was
going to fall at any moment.

She threw herself forward with her
arms outstretched, just as Flame fell. She

just managed to catch him before he crashed to the ground, but she fell onto one of her knees and winced as it twisted awkwardly.

"Oh, Flame. I was so scared you'd be killed," Eve gulped, sprawled on the ground with the kitten in her arms.

Flame blinked up at her gratefully. "Thank you for saving me, Eve," he purred softly. "But you could have hurt yourself. Quickly, put me in your bag so no one can see."

Eve moved slightly and almost screamed as a sickening wave of pain shot up her leg. Biting her lip, she lifted Flame back into her bag, just as a burst of silver sparks crackled in his fur. There was a warm, tingling sensation in her knee and she felt the pain draining away, just as if she had poured it down a sink.

Seconds later, Flame emerged from the bag.

"Thanks, Flame. My knee feels good as new," Eve whispered. She got up with Flame still in her arms and looked around for Darren.

She saw Alison, who had just run into the playground with all the groceries and had grabbed Darren as he shot off the end of the slide. She was as white as a ghost as she hugged her little brother tightly. "Don't you ever run off like that again! I thought you were going to fall right down those stairs!" she said shakily.

Eve went over to Alison. "Is Darren all right?"

Alison nodded. "He's fine. How's Flame?"

"He's all right now," Eve said. She looked at Darren. "It was not okay to run off with Flame like that. You could have hurt him badly."

Darren sniffed and rubbed his eyes. "It wasn't me!" he said defiantly.

"I'm really sorry. Now you see what he's like!" Alison looked hopefully at Eve. "You won't say anything to Mom about him running away, right?"

Eve thought for a moment. Darren definitely wasn't the little angel he first seemed! But it wasn't Alison's fault he ran away. "No, I won't say anything," she decided. "But maybe you should tell your mom how Darren gives you so much trouble."

Alison smiled gratefully. "I'll think about it. Thanks, Eve. You're all right."

★

"Can I go to the movies with Alison tomorrow, Dad?" Eve asked early that evening as she helped make a salad to go with the lasagna her dad was making. Her mom was busy in the office, booking in a new cat, so her dad had offered to cook dinner.

"That sounds like a good idea. You must miss going out with your friends back home," Mr. Dawson said, ruffling her blond hair.

"I was a little at first, when I didn't really know Alison," Eve admitted. "But I do have the best friend anyone could wish for—Flame!"

Flame looked up from his dish of tuna flakes and gave an extra-loud purr.

Her dad chuckled. "I think Flame agrees! And I'm glad you and Alison are getting along now." He paused. "On another subject altogether, that grumpy ginger and white cat didn't eat much food

again. I hope he isn't getting sick."

"Oscar?" Eve guessed.

"He's one of your favorites, isn't he?
I think we'll get him checked out by the
vet." Her dad popped the dinner in the
oven. "I'm just going to the office. I'll get
your mom to call Oscar's owners when
she has a minute, to tell them what's
happening."

Curious, Eve decided she'd go and have a quick look at Oscar herself.

"Come on, Flame," she called as the little kitten padded along behind her.

As soon as she opened Oscar's cage and stepped inside with Flame, the grumpy cat pricked up his ears. Oscar gave a low growl in his throat and then he spotted Flame. His eyes narrowed with interest as he walked over to the kitten and had a good sniff. A moment later, Oscar started purring.

"He seems to like you, Flame," Eve said in amazement. "I wonder if Dad's right about Oscar being sick." She risked petting Oscar gently. He put up with it for a second or two and then moved away. "Poor Oscar. Do you feel okay?

Is that why you're grumpy?" *It's a shame you can't talk like Flame,* she thought. *Then you could tell us what's wrong.*

# Chapter
# *SIX*

"Hooray, it's Saturday! My favorite day!" Eve cried the following morning as she dried her hair after taking a shower.

Flame sat on the bedroom windowsill, washing his face with the side of one front paw. He gave her a whiskery grin. "Why do you like this day so much?"

"Because it's when I get my allowance!" Eve said in a voice muffled by the towel over her head. "And I'm going to the movies!"

Flame frowned. "What is that? It

sounds like a good place."

"Oh, it is. It's where they show moving pictures, called movies. They can be funny or sad or even scary. You can buy popcorn to eat, too. It's so much fun."

Flame's eyes widened. "I would like to see these moving pictures. Will you take me with you?" he purred excitedly.

"Of course I will," Eve promised.
"But you'll have to hide in my bag again."

Flame nodded. "And what is this
popcorn you eat? Is it something like cat
food?"

Eve bit back a grin. "Not exactly. I
think you'll want to pass on the popcorn!"

She finished drying her hair and then
reached for her bag. Flame jumped inside
and curled up.

As she went to call Alison, Eve couldn't
help thinking about Oscar. The vet had
kept him at the office as he wanted to do
some tests.

Alison opened her front door, wearing
just a long baggy T-shirt and slippers.

Eve thought she must have forgotten

about going to the movies. "Hi, Alison! You'd better hurry or we'll miss the start of the movie," she said.

"I'm . . . I'm not coming," Alison gulped. Her eyes looked red and puffy as if she'd been crying. "Darren's been acting up again. Mom got mad and now I'm grounded."

"What's he been up to?" Eve asked.

Alison wiped her eyes. "I was doing my homework in the kitchen when Darren sneaked upstairs. He got a hold of Mom's lipsticks and rubbed them all over the duvets and bedroom curtains. It took Mom hours to get the stains out."

"But that wasn't your fault," Eve said indignantly.

Alison shrugged. "Try telling my mom

that. I explained that Darren slipped
past without me noticing, but she said I
should have checked on him. The little
horror was quiet as a mouse up there.
You know what he's like."

"Yes, I do," Eve said with feeling,
remembering how Darren had run away
with Flame. "I'm really sorry you can't

come out today. Maybe we can go to the movies another time."

Alison nodded and gave her a watery smile. "Yeah, okay," she murmured, before shutting the door.

"Poor Alison. She was really upset," Eve said to Flame as they retraced their steps back to the kennel. "I don't know how she puts up with that little terror of a brother!"

★

"Whose dumb idea was it to volunteer to look after the kennel?" Jim Dawson groaned on Sunday afternoon as he stretched and yawned.

Eve giggled and gave him a playful shove. "Mom's and yours, silly!"

Her dad chuckled. "Well, next time I

have an idea like that, someone shoot me!"

Eve made everyone some hot chocolate. She took a mug in to her dad and then went into the office where her mom was catching up with some paperwork.

"Thanks, honey." Mary Dawson took the hot chocolate and sipped gratefully. "I'm almost finished here. I thought we could all go out for a walk and get some air?"

Eve put her head to one side. "Do you mind if I don't come, Mom? I was planning to watch that new video Dad got for me, since I didn't get to go to the movies with Alison." Eve was looking forward to showing Flame what video and TV were like!

Her mom patted her arm. "No, that's

fine, sweetie. How about you, Jo? Do you and Darren want to come?"

Jo had just popped in to deliver a pile of ironing. Darren was outside the back door, kicking a ball against the terrace wall. Jo smiled. "A walk's probably just what Darren and I need. And it'll give Alison a little peace while she's doing her homework."

Eve was happy that Alison had some peace and quiet for a change, especially after the lipstick disaster. Even though she sometimes felt a little lonely without any brothers or sisters, she didn't envy her having a brother like Darren.

After everyone had left, Eve decided she needed some chips and a drink to go with the movie. She looked in the kitchen cabinet, but they were out of chips. Now that she'd set her heart on them, she didn't want anything else.

"Come on, Flame. We'll just have to go and buy some treats," she said, pulling on a jacket.

It was windy in the street. Yellow and green leaves scuttled by in little whirlwinds along the sidewalk. Flame

couldn't resist them. He ran around,
play-growling and pouncing on leaves,
his sand colored tail wagging from side
to side with excitement.

At the store, Eve bought some
chips and chocolate and a big bottle of
lemonade. As she came back, she passed
Alison's house. On impulse, she decided
to ask Alison if she'd like to come and
watch the movie with her.

"I bet she'll be glad to get away
from doing homework," she said to
Flame as she knocked on the front
door.

Alison took forever to answer the
door. Eve was about to give up when
the door opened a crack.

"Hi," Eve said brightly. "Dad rented

a movie for me. Do you want to come to watch it with Flame and me?"

"Oh, er . . . Hi, Eve," Alison puffed, out of breath.

Her cheeks were pink and her long brown hair was all over the place. Eve noticed there was a Band-Aid on her finger. It looked new, as if Alison had just put it on. "Did you cut your finger?" Eve asked worriedly.

"No! I mean . . . I . . . er . . . burned it on the toaster. Silly, isn't it?" She gave Eve an awkward grin. "A movie sounds great. Thanks. I'll just grab my coat."

Eve raised her eyebrows at Flame. Alison was acting really odd.

Alison reappeared in her coat.

"Ready? Let's go."

Back at the kennel, Eve, Alison, and Flame settled down in the living room. The movie was fun. It was a great fantasy adventure. Flame curled up on Eve's lap, watching it intently and purring loudly.

Alison grinned. "I think that kitten likes movies. It's amazing."

Eve just smiled, thinking that Flame

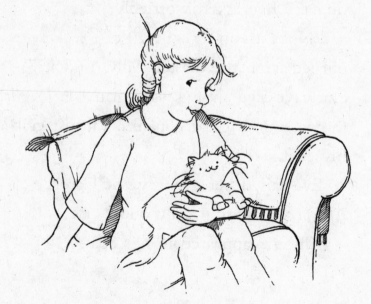

was even more amazing than Alison realized!

As Eve took the movie out of the player, her parents, Jo, and Darren came in. They were all flushed and wind-blown from their walk.

"Can I play in the backyard?" Darren asked.

"I wish I had that boy's energy," Mrs. Dawson said with a smile, going into the kitchen after Darren. "I'll make us all a hot drink."

"What are you doing here, Alison? I thought you were doing your homework," asked Jo, frowning.

"That was my fault," Eve said quickly. "I asked her to come over to watch a movie. That's okay, isn't it?"

Jo's face softened as she smiled at Alison and Eve. "Of course it is. It's nice that you two are spending time together. You can always finish your homework later, Alison."

Alison rolled her eyes at Eve. "Thanks," she whispered. "I thought I was in trouble for a minute there!"

Eve chatted with her dad, Jo, and Alison for a couple of minutes and then decided to go and see if her mom wanted any help. Flame followed her into the kitchen.

"What's that noise, Mom?" Eve said as she heard some scuffling and clanging coming from outside. She looked out of the kitchen window, expecting to see Darren kicking his ball around, but he wasn't on the patio. "It's coming from over the fence. Something's going on near the cages. Come on, Flame. Let's go and take a look."

Her mom frowned. "Wait a minute, sweetie. I'll get your dad."

But Eve and Flame were already rushing through the storeroom and running out into the yard. Eve stopped, her eyes widening with dismay as she saw the terrible mess.

The garbage cans had been tipped over. Newspapers and garbage had spilled everywhere. And right in the middle of the mess was Darren.

# Chapter
# *SEVEN*

Eve's parents and Jo came out into the yard. "Oh, no!" Mr. and Mrs. Dawson gasped.

Jo ran over to Darren. "Bad boy! What possessed you to do this?" she shouted.

Darren looked up at his mom with innocent blue eyes. "It wasn't me!"

Jo bent down in front of her son. "You're only making it worse by telling lies!"

"I'm not!" Darren insisted, sticking out his bottom lip. "It wasn't me."

Jo looked really embarrassed as she turned toward the Dawsons. "I'm really sorry about this! I'll take Darren home and then come back and help clean up this mess. Alison, will you stay at home with him, please?" she called to her daughter who stood in the doorway.

Alison's shoulders slumped and she sighed heavily. "Why me?" she complained. Then she saw her mom's expression. "Okay, if I have to," she said in a small voice.

Darren's angelic face crumpled. He howled in protest as his mom marched him away.

Mrs. Dawson sighed. "Jo seems very upset. I think I'll go inside and talk to her."

"All right," her husband said as he

began picking up sheets of newspapers.
Eve picked up some packets and reached
for a couple of garbage cans. "Careful
you don't cut yourself, honey. Those are
sharp," her dad warned. "You should
put some thick gloves on. Oh, that's the
phone now. I'll be right back."

"Darren is such a pest!" Eve said to Flame. She thought you needed three eyes to watch him—two in the front and one in the back of your head. "This mess is going to take forever to clean up."

Flame gave a short meow. "Do not worry, Eve. I will help you."

Eve felt the familiar tingle up her spine as Flame's sand colored fur ignited with silver sparks and his whiskers crackled and fizzed. Eve couldn't wait to see what would happen next! Flame pointed a tiny paw, his emerald eyes flashing with concentration. Suddenly a comet's tail of glittery light shot all around the garbage-strewn paved area.

*Bang!* The cans stood at attention and opened their lids. *Rustle!* Newspapers rose up high into the sky and then fluttered back down into the bottom of the bins. *Crunch! Clunk!* The packets, boxes, and cans marched one behind the other, like toy soldiers, right up to the garbage can and then shot inside.

Eve clapped her hands in delight as they snapped shut—not a single piece of the mess Darren had made remained. "Thanks, Flame. That was fantastic!"

"You are welcome." Flame sneezed as a final spark tickled his nose and then faded before Eve's eyes.

A few minutes later, Eve's dad came back out into the yard. "Another owner wanting to book their cat in . . ." He broke off in amazement as he noticed that every bit of garbage was gone. "Wow!

How did you manage to clean up so quickly?"

Eve gave him a broad grin. "Oh, I'm full of magic tricks!" *At least, Flame is,* she thought, wishing she could tell everyone how special Flame really was.

★

"That was the vet. He wants to talk about Oscar," Mary Dawson said the following afternoon, hanging up the phone. "I'm going to pop over there now."

"Can Flame and I come with you?" Eve asked eagerly.

"All right," her mom agreed.

"I'll meet you at the car!" Eve jumped up and went to get a bag for Flame.

At the clinic, the receptionist took them straight through to a treatment room. Eve was carrying Flame in her arms. "Hello again," the vet said when he saw Eve and Flame. "Still got his fat little tummy, I see. Good, good."

Eve felt Flame stiffen indignantly and lay his ears flat. A tiny spark tingled against her fingers for a second. "It's okay, Flame, the vet's trying to be nice," she whispered hurriedly to him. "Healthy kittens are supposed to have round tummies."

Flame relaxed and pricked up his ears.

The door opened and a nurse brought Oscar in and put him on the table. Eve put Flame down on the table beside Oscar. Flame meowed softly and rubbed his sand colored head against the older cat's leg. Oscar touched noses with the kitten and began purring softly.

"Hello, boy. How are you?" Eve pet Oscar as she listened to the vet. He explained that Oscar had something with a very long, complicated name, which some cats developed as they grew older.

"But is he going to get better?" Eve asked worriedly.

The vet nodded. "Oh, yes. He got some medicine and he's already feeling much better. Once he gets his appetite back, he'll be just like his old self."

"That's amazing!" Eve exclaimed. She was so happy that Oscar was going to be okay. Flame seemed excited, too, and even seemed to have forgotten to be mad at the vet!

★

Back at the kennel, Eve and Flame took Oscar to his cage and made him comfortable. She discovered some of her dad's favorite shrimp in the kitchen fridge and took a couple as a treat for Oscar. "Here you are, Flame. There's a few for you, too. Dad won't miss them!"

Flame chomped down the shrimp and then licked his lips to get every last fishy taste. "That was delicious. I like this human food!"

The rest of the afternoon passed quickly. Eve helped her dad for a while and then gave Jo a hand cleaning cages with disinfectant. When a delivery of dried cat food arrived from a pet-food supplier, she showed the driver where to put the sacks.

Darren was on his best behavior. He stayed by Alison's side while Jo worked, and even played with Flame. Eve thought he seemed sorry for running away with Flame the other day.

She felt really tired by the time she went upstairs and crawled into bed. Rain pattered against the bedroom window. She drifted slowly off to sleep to the sound of it, with Flame's warm furry little body curled up next to her.

★

Eve woke up with a start.

She sat up, blinking in the darkness, trying to work out what it was that had woken her. She listened carefully. Every now and then, she was sure she could hear faint sounds coming from outside.

"Can you hear that?" she whispered to Flame.

"Yes, I can. Someone is out there," the little kitten meowed softly, jumping across to the windowsill.

Eve's heart beat fast. She got out of bed and peeped through the curtain. It was still raining. The terrace with its table and chairs looked shiny in the darkness. Beyond the terrace wall, the extension and the cat cages looked dim and shadowed.

As the moon slipped out from behind a cloud, Eve froze. The storeroom door leading to the yard was wide open. She watched as a slim, dark figure came out dragging something that looked heavy. It was only then that she noticed the dark humps already lying out on the paved area.

A burglar was stealing the bags of cat food!

"Come on, Flame, we have to stop them!" Eve said, already dashing for the door and racing downstairs in her pajamas.

With Flame running ahead of her, Eve rushed into the extension. A blast of cold air met her as she ran outside. She could see the dark figure a short distance away in the yard, bending over a sack of food. It was wearing dark pants and a top with the hood up.

"Stop, thief!" Eve meant to shout, but it came out as a dry croak. She tried again, this time yelling at the top of her lungs. "STOP, THIEF!!"

"Wha . . . !" The figure almost jumped out of its skin with shock. It straightened

up and started hurrying toward the gate
at the side of the house.

Eve didn't think twice. She ran
after the burglar, but Flame was even
faster. He hurtled toward the gate and

scrambled up it until he stood balanced on the top. His sand colored fur bristled as he arched his tiny back. Hissing fiercely, he faced the burglar.

Eve's heart hammered in her chest. Flame was so brave. She could imagine just what he would be like as a Lion Prince, even though here he couldn't use any magic or he'd give himself away. Eve was so scared.

The hooded figure raced up to the gate and grabbed the latch. "Get off! Go away!" the burglar shouted at Flame.

Eve's eyes widened in shock. It was a girl's voice! One she recognized.

Flame recognized the burglar, too. He gave a loud whine and jumped into the girl's arms. The burglar took a step backward, holding Flame. She turned around slowly to face Eve as Eve pushed back her hood.

"Alison!"

# Chapter
# *EIGHT*

Eve sat with Flame huddled inside her dad's fleece jacket. Her bare feet stuck out of her rain-soaked pajama bottoms. From the look in her dad's eyes, she knew she was in for a scolding for running outside in the middle of the night by herself.

At least the cat food hadn't gotten too wet. It was all back inside the storeroom and her mom had assured everyone that it would be fine.

Alison sat opposite Eve, looking

shamefaced. Mr. and Mrs. Dawson sat on either side of her.

"But why, Alison?" Mrs. Dawson asked gently. "What did you hope to gain by stealing the cat food?"

"I wasn't stealing it. I just wanted it to get wet, so everyone would be furious with Darren. You were supposed to think he'd dragged the food out," Alison said miserably.

Eve's dad looked at his wife. "Am I missing something?"

Eve thought she was beginning to work it out. "You wanted everyone to see what hard work Darren really was?" she said to Alison, remembering the supermarket.

Alison nodded. "I wanted Mom to see, so that she would have to take care

of Darren and it wouldn't just be up to me to watch him all the time. But she wouldn't listen."

Flame gave a little meow of sympathy and brushed against Alison's ankle. She leaned down to pet him.

Mr. and Mrs. Dawson looked at each other in amazement.

Something else fell into place for Eve. She remembered the day when she went to Alison's house with the movie. Alison had been really out of breath when she'd answered the door. Then there was the Band-Aid on her finger.

"You didn't burn your finger, did you? You cut it when you tipped all the garbage out!" Eve burst out. "No wonder you were out of breath. You had just rushed back home when I knocked on your front door!"

Alison hung her head, nodding. "Eve's right. I tipped over the garbage so that Darren would get blamed. I know I've been really stupid. Are . . . are you going to call the police?"

Her mom and dad looked at each other.

Eve stared at her parents in horror. "You aren't going to, are you? They'll probably handcuff Alison and throw her into a cell. And she'll only get bread and water to eat . . ."

"That's enough, Eve," her dad said with a faint smile. "I think it's time we took Alison home and I had a word with her mom." He gave Eve a firm, direct look. "And as for you, young lady, you can go straight back to bed."

Eve knew when her dad meant business. She rose to her feet and then picked up Flame. "Okay," she said in a subdued voice.

Alison looked back from the doorway, her eyes bright with tears. "I'm really sorry for what I've done. Will you still be friends with me, Eve?"

Eve only hesitated for a second. "Of course I will. And Flame will, too."

★

"Jo was pretty surprised and upset when she heard about what Alison had been up to," Mrs. Dawson told Eve the following morning. "But Alison seems genuinely sorry. She's even offered to buy Darren the toy car he wants with her allowance. I persuaded Jo that no real harm was done. She decided to make sure Alison has more time for herself, without Darren tagging along, too. I think the whole thing will soon blow over."

"That's amazing! Good work, Mom," Eve said warmly. Her mom was really good at calming people down.

"But as for you, young lady . . ." her dad said.

"I know!" Eve said quickly.

She still felt really guilty for worrying her parents. Her dad said he couldn't believe his eyes when he'd seen her in her pajamas, chasing what appeared to be a burglar!

"I've already promised Mom that I won't ever, ever, ever do anything like that again," she said, making cross-my-heart movements with one finger. "And I really mean it."

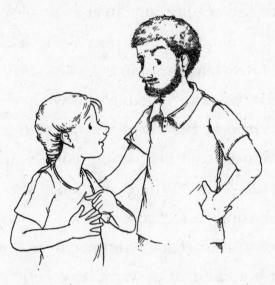

"I'm sure you do. Until next time?" her dad said with a twinkle in his eye. "Let's forget all about it. Where's Flame this morning? He usually follows you everywhere."

"I know." Eve felt an odd little pang. Flame had been strangely reluctant to come downstairs with her. She had left him curled up on her duvet.

"I'll go and get him now," she said, walking toward the stairs.

"Flame?" Eve called as she went into her bedroom. But there was no sign of him. She looked behind the curtain and under the bed. "Where are you?" she said, starting to feel anxious.

There was a faint whimper from beneath a chest of drawers. Eve bent down. She saw Flame crouched right at the back against the wall.

"What's wrong, Flame?"

"My enemies are getting near. I can sense them," he yowled worriedly. He crawled out slowly, keeping his tummy low to the ground. His big green eyes were huge and scared.

Eve picked him up. As she pet Flame's long, sand colored fur, she felt his tiny body trembling. "It's okay. You're safe with me. You . . . you don't have to leave, do you?" she asked hesitantly. "I'll take care of you, I promise."

She had been looking forward so much to taking Flame home with her.

Flame shook his head. "Not yet. But if my uncle's spies come any closer, then I must leave at once."

Eve held him close. She rubbed her chin gently on the top of his little head. "I don't want you to go. I want you to stay with me forever," she whispered, refusing to think of losing her special friend.

Flame purred softly, but his emerald eyes remained troubled.

# Chapter
# *NINE*

"It's our last day at the kennel.
Sally will be back tonight. And we're all
going home early tomorrow. Including
you!" Eve told Flame excitedly.

Flame seemed more relaxed and the
fearful look had faded from his eyes.
Eve hoped that Flame's enemies were
hundreds of miles away. It was too
painful to think of going home
without him.

"Should we go and see Oscar?" she
suggested, deciding to change the subject.

Flame gave an eager little meow. "Yes, I would like that." He ran along beside Eve, his silky tail sticking up in excitement.

Oscar was sitting, having a bath. As soon as he saw Eve and Flame, he came trotting over. Eve let herself into the cage and crouched down to pet the big ginger and white cat. Flame purred and licked Oscar's ears. Eve smiled as Oscar rubbed his head against the tiny kitten.

"Are we friends now then, Oscar?" Eve said. "You're not really grumpy, are you, boy? You were just sick and a bit lonely."

After she closed Oscar's cage, she went to tell her mom about his progress.

Mrs. Dawson was on the office phone.

"That's such a shame. But I understand.
Poor Oscar. I've got a couple of numbers
I can call. I'll let you know what
happens. Good-bye."

"What's wrong?" Eve asked.

Her mom frowned. "Oscar's owners
were very upset. They just found out
they have to move because of their work.

There's a strict rule that no pets are
allowed, so it looks like Oscar might have
to find a new home."

"Oh, no," Eve said, feeling upset. It
didn't seem fair after all poor Oscar had
been through.

She tried not to think about Oscar
as she helped with the usual chores, but
she couldn't seem to get him out of her
mind.

Jo, Darren, and Alison had come in
early. With Sally coming back, everyone
was working extra hard to have the
kennel looking its best.

Alison had a quiet word with Eve.
"Mom's been great about everything.
She says I won't need to help out with
Darren as much when Sally's back. And

Darren's going to be starting nursery school in a few weeks, so he'll be happier, too." She grinned. "He'll have lots more kids to run around and be mischievous with!"

As Eve helped with the last few chores, she felt a bit sad. She was going to miss taking care of all the cats, especially Oscar. Then she brightened up; having Flame with her was going to be fantastic. She couldn't wait to show him to all her friends.

Her dad came in as Eve was stacking clean food dishes into a cabinet. "In a few hours, we'll be on our way. Who would have thought that we'd be taking *two* cats home with us?"

Eve stared blankly at him. "Two cats?

Flame and . . . ?" Suddenly she realized
what her dad was saying. "Oscar!"

"Yes, Oscar!" her dad said, laughing at
the happy expression on her face. "We're
adopting him. Your mom and I can see
that you really care about him."

Eve felt a warm glow in her chest.
"Do you really mean it?" She flung her

arms around her dad. "That's wonderful!"

She rushed off to tell Flame the good news. He was going to be so happy. She had left him sniffing around in the yard in front of the cat cages.

Flame looked up and meowed a greeting as she came toward him.

Suddenly Eve glimpsed fierce, shadowy cat shapes behind Flame. They were peering into the cages. Her heart missed a beat.

"Flame, look out!" she cried.

Acting on instinct, she grabbed the water hose used to wash out the cages. Turning it on, she aimed a jet of water at Flame's enemies. The cat shapes slunk back, trying to avoid a soaking.

There was a flash of dazzling bright

light. Flame was no longer a tiny, sand colored kitten, but instead stood in front of Eve as a magnificent, young, white lion once more. At his side this time was an older adult, gray lion.

Flame lifted his regal head and looked at Eve with sad green eyes. "Be well, Eve," he growled in a deep, velvety voice. He raised a large, white paw in

120

farewell and then was gone.

There was a terrifying howl of rage from the fierce dark cats, before they, too, disappeared.

Eve stood alone in the yard. A deep sadness welled up in her. She couldn't believe Flame had had to go so suddenly. She was relieved that Flame was safe, but she was going to miss him so much.

"I'll never forget you, Flame," she whispered as her eyes prickled with tears. She knew that she would always treasure the time she had shared with the tiny magic kitten.

Wiping her eyes, she turned around and went toward Oscar's cage as she thought about how to tell her mom and dad. Somehow she knew that Flame was watching with a smile of approval in his big emerald eyes.

# *About the Author*

Sue Bentley's books for children often include animals or fairies. She lives in Northampton and enjoys reading, going to the movies, and watching the frogs and newts in her garden pond. If she hadn't been a writer, she would probably have been a skydiver or a brain surgeon. The main reason she writes is that she can drink pots and pots of tea while she's typing. She has met and owned many cats and each one has brought a special sort of magic to her life.